What Happens Next?

Bill Gillham

Photographs by Jan Siegieda

G. P. Putnam's Sons New York

Chicken in a nest . . .
what happens next?

A lovely warm egg!

Down comes the rain . . .
what happens next?

Splashing in puddles!

The baby is crying . . .
what happens next?

Mommy gives him a bottle!

Make a sandcastle . . .
what happens next?

The sea comes in and washes it away!

Build the tower higher and higher . . .
what happens next?

It all falls down!

Press the button on the box . . .
what happens next?

Up pops Jack!

Fill up the watering can . . .
what happens next?

Give the flowers some water!

Make a birthday cake . . .
what happens next?

Blow out the candles!

Hang up a bird feeder . . .
what happens next?

The bird eats the nuts!

Pour in the bubble bath . . .
what happens next?

Play with the bubbles!

Flags, rope and wood . . .
what happens next?

A tree house to play in!

Feed the goldfish . . .
what happens next?

Watch them gobble!

Daddy blows up a balloon . . .
what happens next?

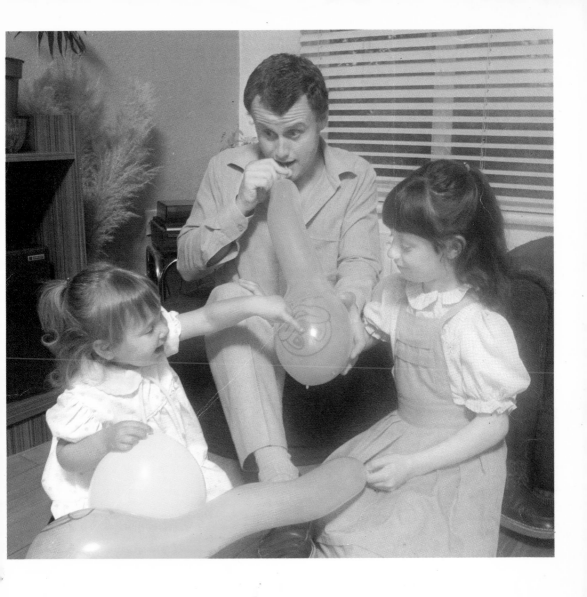

What a funny face!

Look inside the box . . .
what happens next?

A special present!

It's starting to snow . . .
what happens next?

Make a snowman!

In this book, as in Bill Gillham's earlier books, children are encouraged to look at the world around them, and to think and talk about what they see. Not only will they develop their powers of thought and language by answering the question, "What happens next?" but they will gain additional pleasure from sharing the book with adults.

Dr. Bill Gillham, a leading educational psychologist at Strathclyde University in Scotland, is the author of *The First Words Picture Book, The Early Words Picture Book, Let's Look for Colors, Let's Look for Numbers, Let's Look for Opposites* and *Let's Look for Shapes.*

Jan Siegieda is a freelance photographer who has previously worked with Bill Gillham on the *Let's Look* books.

Text copyright © 1985 Bill Gillham
Photographs copyright © 1985 Bill Gillham and Jan Siegieda
First American edition 1985
First published by Methuen Children's Books, Ltd, London, England.

Library of Congress Cataloging in Publication Data

Gillham, Bill.
　What happens next?

　Summary: Pairs of photographs present questions and answers which explore some causes and effects in a child's world. Example: "Down comes the rain . . . what happens next? Splashing in puddles!"
　1. Children's questions and answers. 2. Causation – Juvenile literature. [1. Questions and answers] I. Siegieda, Jan, ill. II. Title.
AG195.G5　1985　　031′.02　　　84-26293
ISBN 0-399-21255-8
First printing
　Printed in Great Britain